# GEORGE SHRINKS

# GEORGE SHRINKS

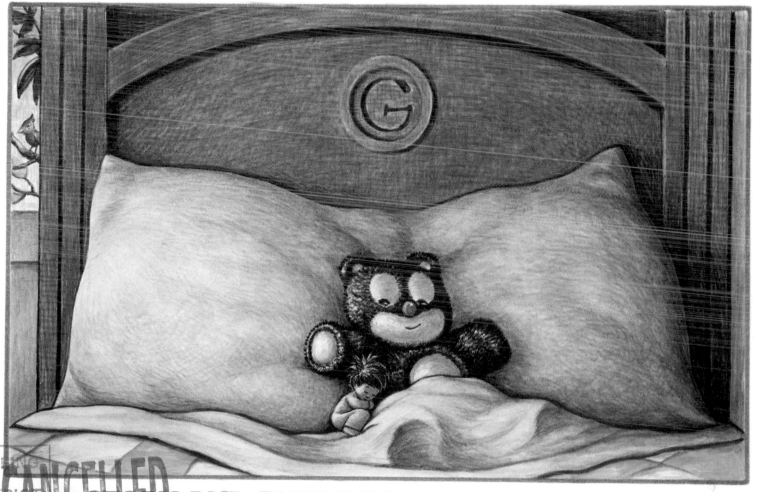

STORY AND PICTURES BY WILLIAM JOYCE

LONDON · VICTOR GOLLANCZ LTD · 1986

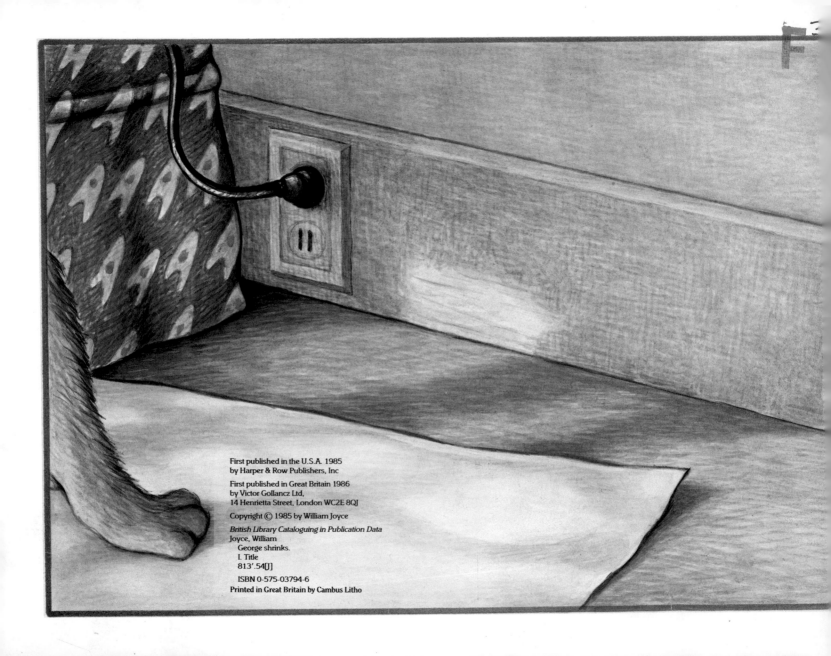

First published in the U.S.A. 1985
by Harper & Row Publishers, Inc

First published in Great Britain 1986
by Victor Gollancz Ltd,
14 Henrietta Street, London WC2E 8QJ

Copyright © 1985 by William Joyce

*British Library Cataloguing in Publication Data*
Joyce, William.
  George shrinks.
  I. Title
  813'.54[J]

  ISBN 0-575-03794-6

**Printed in Great Britain by Cambus Litho**

One day, while his mother and father were out,
George dreamt he was small,
and when he woke up he found it was true.

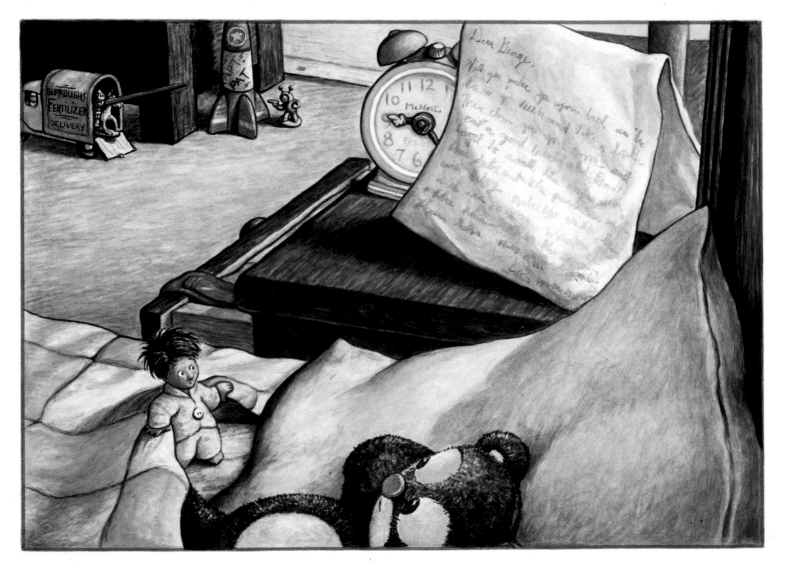

His parents had left him a note:

"Dear George," it said. "When you wake up,

please make your bed,

brush your teeth,

and have a bath.

Then tidy your room

and wake up your little brother.

Eat a good breakfast,

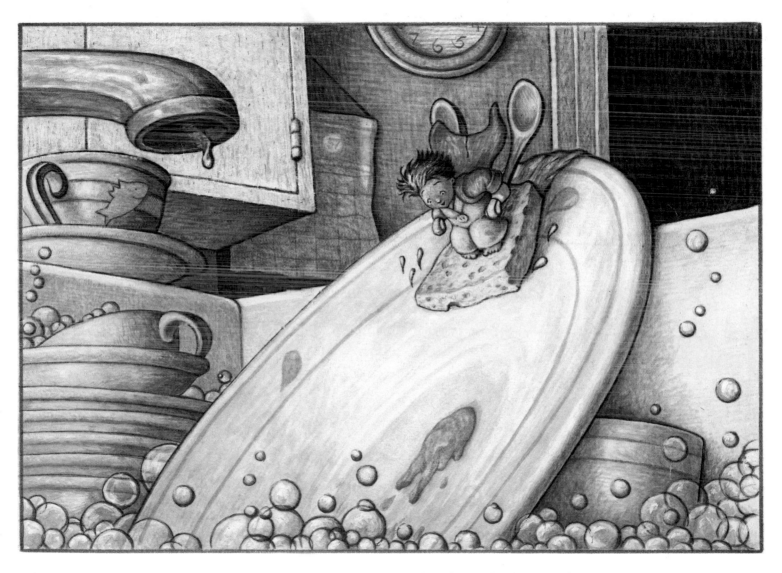

and don't forget to wash the dishes, dear.

Take out the rubbish,

and play quietly.

Make sure you water the plants

and feed the fish.

Then check the post

and get some fresh air.

Try to stay out of trouble,

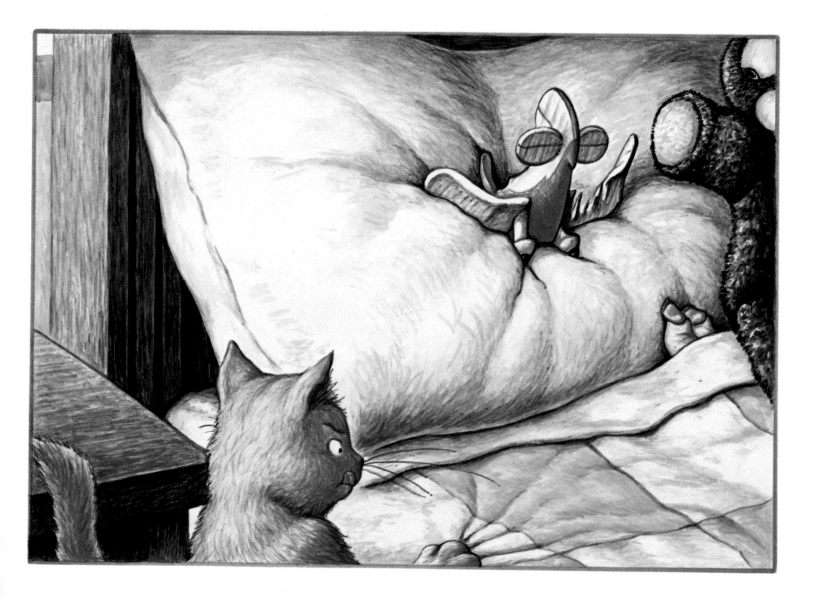

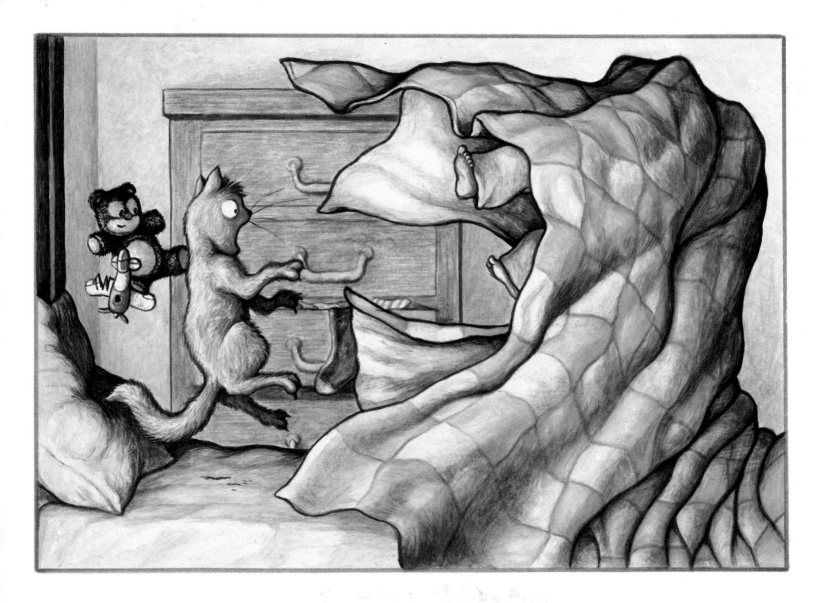

and we'll be home soon.

Love, Mum and Dad."